Chekhov
Scenes

Monologues & Duologues for Women

Compiled & Edited by Kim Gilbert

Copyright © 2020 Kim Gilbert
All rights reserved.
ISBN: 9798644539277

DEDICATION

This collection of Chekhovian scenes, is dedicated to all students of drama and those readers with a love of one of the greatest short story writers to have ever lived – Anton Chekhov. Continue to explore his works. I hope you gain as much satisfaction from them as I have.

ACKNOWLEDGEMENTS

A special thanks goes to my husband Steve, who has prepared this collection for publication, and has bailed me out on numerous occasions over the years, with his technical expertise.

TABLE OF CONTENTS

Introduction   1
About Chekhov   3

MONOLOGUES

Ivanov   7

The Seagull   17

Uncle Vanya   27

Three Sisters   37

The Cherry Orchard   49

My Life   55

A Marriage Proposal   57

The Brute   59

The Anniversary   63

DUOLOGUES

Uncle Vanya   69

The Cherry Orchard   73

Three Sisters   76

About the Author   81

INTRODUCTION

I have compiled and edited this collection of Chekhovian monologues for young female actors to study as well as enjoy. This book is equally useful as a teaching aid for teachers of acting. These classical scenes are suitable for a range of acting exams and awards as well as for auditions and festivals. I have tried and tested these scenes with numerous students over the years with great success and more importantly, they have thoroughly enjoyed working on them. The monologues & duologues in this collection are taken from a range of Chekhov's plays, one act farces and short stories: The Three Sisters, The Cherry Orchard, The Seagull, Uncle Vanya, Ivanov and others. There is a short biography on Chekhov, some notes about his writing style and a short synopsis of each play. Each scene has an introduction suitably prepared for exam or festival work. I hope you enjoy this collection.

Chekhov Scenes

ANTON PAVLOVIC CHEKHOV
29th January 1860 - 15th July 1904

Anton Chekhov trained and qualified as a medical doctor and worked as a doctor for all of his life. He started writing stories to support his income. This was due to the fact that he treated many poor patients who could not pay for their medical treatment. Chekhov had 5 sons and was the main breadwinner for his large family. His father also had many debts and Chekhov helped him out financially to avoid his father being sent to Debtors prison. Chekhov wrote over 400 short stories and it is claimed that he is one of the world's greatest writers of short stories. He wrote stories of contemporary Russian life. Chekhov suffered from tuberculosis for most of his life and it was this disease that eventually killed him in 1904, whilst he was living in Germany.

Chekhov wrote in the style of realism, a literary technique which describes locations, characters and themes in a realistic style without using elaborate imagery or rhetorical language. Literary realism emerged in the nineteenth century in France and was a popular modernist movement. The subjects and themes were of ordinary recognisable people that his readers could identify with. His writing style is also described as impressionistic realism. This means that the emotions of the characters evoke a certain vivid and sensory impression rather than creating an objective reality. Chekov is considered a master of realism.

His four major works are his plays: The Seagull, Uncle Vanya, The Three Sisters, and The Cherry Orchard. His play 'Ivanov' was based on an earlier play named 'The Wood Demon'.

His three most popular plays, The Seagull, The Three Sisters and The Cherry Orchard were produced at Stanislavski's Moscow Arts Theatre. Chekhov was a shareholder in this theatre. Chekhov took a lot of persuasion to have his plays staged at the theatre as they had previously been publicly criticised. However, the plays enjoyed great success and marked the beginning of a great partnership between Constantin Stanislavski and Anton Chekhov. The three plays produced at the Moscow Arts made Chekhov into a famous, world renowned playwright. His realistic portrayal of characters and their situations, their emotions and realistic dialogue along with his observation of small talk in provincial middleclass situations made him popular and influenced the writing style of many modernist writers to come.

Chekhov Scenes

The Scenes

Chekhov Scenes

Chekhov Scenes

IVANOV

Nikolai Ivanov is a depressive yet charismatic man. He is no longer in love with his Jewish wife, Anna Petrovna and he has incurred a lot of debt. Anna is terminally ill with tuberculosis and is being cared for by a Doctor Lvov. The doctor suggests that Anna take a trip to recover from her illness but there are not sufficient funds. Ivanov is accused of neglecting his wife in favour of socialising with his boss, Lebvedev and running up debts. It is a common belief that Ivanov married Anna for her wealth. Anna has now lost everything. She sacrificed all ties with her Jewish family in order to marry Ivanov. Ivanov's boss, Lebvedev, has a daughter named Sasha and she has fallen in love with the enigmatic Ivanov. She feels she can cure him of his depression. She pursues a relationship with Ivanov. Anna discovers the affair and confronts her husband. Sasha realizes that Ivanov's wife is terminally ill and eventually, after being discovered, agrees to wait for him until he is in a position to marry her. A year later, Anna dies and Ivanov prepares to marry Sasha. Sasha, has to try to convince those around her that their relationship will survive and the marriage should go ahead. Lvov, the doctor, who was so fond of Anna, is convinced that Ivanov is after Sacha's dowry. He spreads rumours to all who will hear. Consequently, Lvov is challenged to a duel by Ivanov's supporters. At first, Ivanov mocks the whole situation but on contemplating this to be a hopeless case, takes a gun and, despite Sasha's pleas, flees and shoots himself.

Chekov Scenes

Chekov Scenes

IVANOV ACT 1

(Ivanov's wife, Anna, is with Shabelsky and her husband, Nicholas Ivanov. Ivanov spends most of his time away from the house nowadays and Anna is concerned about this).

Anna:
(To Shabelsky)
Leave him alone. Let him alone, Let him go if he enjoys it.

(To Ivanov)
Don't keep making excuses. Just go, no one's keeping you.

Nicholas, do stay at home, dear. We'll talk as we used to. We'll have supper together and read. The old boy and I've learnt a lot of duets for you. *(She puts her arms around him).* Do stay. *(Pause).* I simply don't understand you, this has been going on a whole year. Why have you changed?

Why don't you want me to go out with you at night?
You're depressed, you say. That I understand. Look, Nicholas, why not try singing, laughing and losing your temper, as in the old days. You stay in. We'll laugh, drink home-made wine and cheer you up in no time. Shall I sing? Or shall we go and sit in your study in the dark as we used to, and you can tell me all about how depressed you are. Your eyes are so full of suffering. I'll look into them and cry and we'll both feel better. What is it, Nicholas? Flowers come around every spring, but happiness doesn't – is that it? All right, go then.

IVANOV ACT 1 SC 7

(Anna is talking to her doctor and friend, Eugene Lvov, about the state of her marriage to Nicholas Ivanov).

Anna:
Doctor, why are you striding about there? Come and sit down here.

Flowers come round every spring, but happiness doesn't. Who told me that? Now let me see, I think Nicholas himself said it.

I'm beginning to think I've been unlucky, Doctor. There are lots of people, no better than me perhaps, who are happy and whose happiness costs them nothing. But I've paid for everything, every single thing. And so dearly. Why charge me such a shocking rate of interest? My dear, you're all so careful with me, so very tactful, you're afraid to tell me the truth, but do you think I don't know what's the matter with me? I know all right. Anyway, it's a boring subject.

I've also started wondering why people are so unfair. Why can't they love those who love them? Why do they have to lie when they're told the truth? Tell me, when will my mother and father stop hating me? They live nearly forty miles away, but I feel their hatred all day and night, even in my sleep. And what am I to make of Nicholas being so depressed? He says it's only when he's bored stiff in the evenings that he doesn't love me. I understand that, I can accept it. But what if he stops loving me altogether? Of course, that can't happen, but – what if it does? No, I mustn't even think of it. What horrible thoughts I have. You're not married, Doctor, so there's a lot you can't understand.

You say Nicholas is this and that and the other. What do you know about him? Can you get to know someone in six months? He's a wonderful man, Doctor, and I'm only sorry you didn't know him a year or two ago. How he's rather under the weather and doesn't speak or do anything. But in the old days – oh, he was so charming, I fell in love at first sight. *(She laughs).* I took one look and snap went the mousetrap! He said we should go away. I cut off everything, you know, like snipping off dead leaves with some scissors, and followed him. *(Pause).* But now things are different. He visits the Lebedevs to enjoy other women's company now, while I – sit in the garden and listen to the howl hooting.

I can't bear it, Doctor.

IVANOV ACT 3 SC 9

(Anna is talking to her husband, Ivanov. She is still in love with him and feels he has betrayed her badly)

Anna:
Why did she come here? *(Pause)*. I ask you – why did she come?

What was she doing here? *(Pause)*. So, this is what you're like! Now I understand – at last I see the kind of man you are, you rotten cad. Remember coming and telling me lies, saying how you loved me? I believed you, gave up my parents and my religion and married you. You lied about truth and goodness and your noble plans, and I believed every word.

I've lived with you five years, I've been depressed and ill, but I loved you and never left your side. I idolized you. And then what? All that time you were blatantly deceiving me.
Now it all makes sense. You married me, thinking my parents would forgive me and give me money. That's what you thought. Shut up! Seeing there was no money in the offing, you started another little game. Now it all comes back, now I see. (*She weeps*) You never loved me, were never faithful to me. Never! You rotten contemptible creature. You're in debt to Lebedev, and now you try to wriggle out of paying by turning his daughter's head and deceiving her as you did me. Well, aren't you? You've always been a barefaced swindler, I'm not the only victim. You pretended all these frauds were Borkin's doing, but I know now who was behind them.

I will not shut up, you've made a fool of me too long, I won't be quiet any more. Now go and make a fool of Sasha Lebedev.

IVANOV ACT 2

(*Sasha is defending Ivanov. People have been making claims against him regarding the recent cattle epidemic. They claim that Ivanov bought cows and once he had insured them, infected them with the plague and collected the insurance money*)

Sasha:

How have you the heart to say all that about a man who hasn't done you any harm? Tell me, what harm has he done you?

Oh, but all this is sheer nonsense! Utter rubbish! No one ever dreamed of buying cattle or infecting cattle! Borkin invented the idea himself and went boasting about it everywhere. When Ivanov found it out, Borkin had to beg his forgiveness for a whole fortnight afterwards. Ivanov's only fault is weakness of character, so that he hasn't the heart to turn that Borkin out. And then he trusts people too much! He's had everything stolen and plundered from him; anyone who felt inclined could make money out of his generosity.

But why do they talk such nonsense? And how boring it all is! Ivanov, Ivanov, Ivanov – there's no other topic of conversation. I'm simply astonished! I'm simply astonished at your patience. Aren't you bored to be sitting here like this? The very air is stiff with boredom! Well, say something, try to entertain the young ladies, do something! If you've nothing else to talk about except Ivanov, can't you laugh, or sing, or dance, or something? …

Listen then, just do me this favour. If you don't want to dance, or sing, or laugh, if all that bored you, then just for once in your life, as an exception, I mean, do try to make a tremendous effort and think of something witty and brilliant to say, something to amuse us. It doesn't matter if it's rude and impertinent, so long as it's funny and novel. Or if you could all do something, something quite small, hardly noticeable, but something a bit original and daring, so that we young ladies could look at you and say 'Oh', admiringly, for once in our lives! You do want to be popular with us, don't you? … Then why don't you try to make us admire you? Oh, you gentlemen! You're a poor lot, a poor lot, all of you! I've told you a thousand times, and I'll go on telling you, too – you're a poor lot!

IVANOV ACT 3

(Sasha has been having an affair with the older, married, depressive Ivanov. At this point in the scene, she pays a visit to his house as she has not seen him for some time)

SASHA:

I'm here! How are you? Weren't you expecting me? Why haven't you been to see us for so long?

Your wife won't see me. I came in through the back door. I'll go in a minute.

What was I to do? You haven't been to see us for a fortnight, you never answered my letters. I've been worn out with worry.

You to blame? Are you to blame because you've stopped loving your wife? A man isn't master of his feelings; you didn't want to stop loving her. Are you to blame because she saw me telling you I loved you? No, you didn't want her to see it …

You're angry with me, it was stupid of me to come here.

There are a lot of things men don't understand. Every girl is more attracted by a man who's a failure than by one who's a success, because what she wants is active love … Men are taken up with their work and so love has to take a back seat with them. To have a talk with his wife, to take a stroll with her in the garden, to pass time pleasantly with her, to weep a little on her grave – But for us – love is life. I love you, and that means that I dream about how I'd cure you of your depression, how I'd follow you to the end of the world … It would be sheer happiness for me to copy out your papers all night long, or watch over you all night so that no one woke you… I remember once you came to our house about three years ago at harvest time, and you were all covered in dust and tired out, and you asked for a drink of water. I went to get you a glass, but you were lying on the sofa, sound asleep, when I came back with it. You slept the best part of the day in our house, and I stood outside the door all the time and guarded it, so that no one should come in. And I was so happy! The greater the effort, the greater the love …

It's time I went. Good-bye! I'm afraid your honest doctor may tell your wife about my being here. Go to your wife now and stay with her … Do your duty. Experience the grief of it, ask her forgiveness, weep – that's just as it should be. But the main thing is – don't forget your work!

God bless you, Nikolai! You needn't think about me! If you write to me in about a fortnight – I'll be grateful for that. I'll write to you … Goodbye, Nikolai.

IVANOV ACT 4

(Borkin has just challenged Ivanov to a duel. Sasha defends him)

Sasha:
What is this? Why do you insult him? Just a moment, everyone, let him tell me – why?

What can you say? That you're an honest man? That's hardly a secret! You'd better tell me frankly whether you know what you're doing or not. You come in here with honest man written over you, terribly insult him and nearly kill me. Before that you've dogged his footsteps and made his life a misery, quite convinced you were doing your duty as an honesty man. You've meddled in his private life, made his name dirt and set yourself up to judge him. You took every chance to bombard me and all his friends with anonymous letters – thinking all the time what a very honest man you were. In the name of honesty you, a doctor, didn't spare even his sick wife, you pestered her with your suspicions. There's no outrageous, rotten, cruel trick you couldn't play while still thinking yourself an unusually honest and progressive man.

Do you know what you're doing, or don't you? Stupid, callous people. Come away, Nicholas. Come on, Father!

(Ivanov takes out his revolver)

(Sasha shrieks) I know what he wants to do. Nicholas, for God's sake!

Nicholas, for God's sake! Stop him!

(Ivanov runs off and shoots himself. The play ends)

Chekhov Scenes

THE SEAGULL

This play in four acts, takes place on a country estate owned by Irina Arkadina's brother, Sorin. The household is a busy one with many characters coming and going. The estate is set at the side of a lake and there is a theatre in the grounds where Irina's son, Konstantin, stages his play and asks his love interest, Nina, to act in it. Konstantin is a misunderstood character. He attempts to create and develop a new form of symbolist writing. Only his Uncle Sorin has sympathy and understanding of him and Dr Dorn is supportive of his writing.

The four main characters in the play are the fading actress, Irina Arkadina, and her writer partner, Boris Trigorin, Irina's playwright son, Konstantin Treplyov and the girl he is in love with, a young actress named Nina.

However, Nina is not really in love with Konstantin despite being fond of him. She does become infatuated with Treplyov, the older and more established writer and partner of Irina Arkadina. Masha a depressed young woman, who drinks too much, is in love with Konstantin. This love is unrequited and Masha eventually settles by marrying the schoolteacher, Medvedenko. The title of the play comes from the part of the play when Konstantin shoots a seagull and gives it to Nina. Trigorin arrives at this moment and suggests this would make the subject of a short story. He likens Nina to the seagull who wishes to be free. Madame Arkadina decides to leave for Moscow after an argument with Shamrayev, the manager of the estate. She takes Trigorin with her although he has recently developed a crush on Nina. Konstantin spends most of his time in a depressive state and in Act 3 he shoots himself in the head. The injury is not life threatening but his head remains bandaged for the rest of Act 3. When Trigorin leaves with Irina, Nina confesses to him that she will also be running away to Moscow in order to pursue her career as an actress.

Two years later during Act 4, Masha has married the school teacher and now has a child. Konstantin has become a good writer. During the lapse in time, Nina has had an affair with Trigorin and has also had a child with him. Unfortunately the child

Chekhov Scenes

died. Eventually, Trigorin and Irina Arkadina reunite. Nina eventually returns to her hometown, older, wiser and disillusioned. Uncle Sorin's health is failing so Irina and Trigorin also return to the lakeside estate. Konstantin begs Nina to stay with him as he is still in love with her but Nina tells him she must leave. Konstantin tears up his latest manuscript, leaves the estate and shoots himself.

THE SEAGULL ACT 1

(Irina Arkadin (Mrs Treplev) is an actress with a son, Constantine Treplev, who has aspirations of being a writer. Constantine has just staged a play and his narcissistic mother has criticised it and he is upset. His uncle Sorin, Medvendenko, Dr Dorn, Polina and Masha are all in this scene and have formed part of the audience at the theatre by the lake).

Irina:
What's up with him? What did I do?

But he told us his play was a joke, and that's just how I treated it. Now he turns out to have written a masterpiece. Oh, for heaven's sake! I suppose he put on this performance, and choked us with sulphur, not as a joke, but to prove a point. He wanted to show us how to write and act. I've really had about enough of this! These constant outbursts and digs against me – well, say what you like, but they'd try anyone's patience. He's a selfish, spoilt little boy.

But of course, he couldn't choose an ordinary play, we have to sit through this experimental rubbish. Now, I don't mind listening to rubbish for a laugh, but doesn't this stuff claim to be a new art form, something epoch-making? Well, I don't see any new art form here, just a display of bad manners. Let him write what he likes as best he can, but leave me out of it. I'm not annoyed, I'm only sorry to see a young man spend his time so tediously. I didn't mean to hurt his feelings.
(She sits)

It's such a heavenly evening. Ten or fifteen years ago there was music and singing by this lake almost every night. There are six estates on the shore. There was so much laughter, fun and shooting, I remember, and so many, many love affairs. But who was the darling and idol of all six estates? I present our doctor, Eugene Dorn. He's still charming, but in those days he was irresistible. Still, I'm beginning to feel rather guilty. Why did I hurt my poor boy's feelings? I'm worried. *(Loudly)* Constantine, my dear! Constantine!

THE SEAGULL ACT 2

(On the lawn near the lake, Irina is talking to 22 yr old Masha who is a depressive and Dr Dorn who is reading a book)

Irina:

Let's stand up. Side by side. You're twenty-two and I'm nearly twice as old. Now, Dr Dorn, which of us looks younger? Me, of course. Andy why? Because I work, I feel I'm always on the go, while you just stay put – you're only half alive. And I make it a rule not to look into the future, I never think of growing old or dying. What is to be will be.

Then again I'm most particular, dear, like an Englishman. I keep myself in trim and my clothes and hair are always just right. Do I ever go out, even in the garden, with my housecoat on, without doing my hair? No, I don't. That's why I've lasted so well, because I've never been slovenly and let myself go like some I could mention. *(She strolls up and down the garden).*

See what I mean? Just like a dear little robin. I could play a girl of fifteen.

(She sits down next to Dr Dorn who is reading)

You read. Or rather let me have it, I'll read, it's my turn. *(She takes the books and finds the page).* 'And the rats". Here we are. *(She reads from the book)* 'For society people to encourage novelists and make a fuss of them is as obviously dangerous as for a corn-dealer to let rats breed in his storerooms. But you see, writers are very popular. So when a woman's marked one down for capture, she keeps on at him, flattering him, being nice to him and spoiling him.' Well, the French may be like that, but we're different, we don't have things so cut and dried. Before a Russian woman tries to ensnare a writer she's usually head over heels in love with him, believe me. No need to look far – take me and Trigorin.

THE SEAGULL ACT 3

(Irina and Trigorin are planning to leave the estate. She wants to get back to the city where she can resume her life on the stage. Irina also feels that Trigon has become a little too fond of Nina).

<u>Irina Arkadin:</u>
The carriage will be here soon. I hope all your things are packed?

I know why you want to stay, dear, but you must pull yourself together. You're a little intoxicated, so sober down. Are you so infatuated? The love of a little provincial miss? How little you know yourself.

Don't torture me, Boris, I'm terrified.

Am I really so old and ugly that you don't mind talking to me about other women? (*She embraces and kisses him*). Oh, you're mad. My marvellous, splendid man. You're the last page in my life. (*She kneels to him*). My delight, my pride, my joy! If you leave me for one hour I shan't survive, I shall go mad, my wonderful, splendid one. My master.

I'm not ashamed of loving you. *(She kisses his hands)*. My dear, reckless boy, you want to do something crazy, but I won't have it, I won't let you. You're mine, mine. This forehead's mine, these eyes are mine, this lovely silky hair's mine too. You're mine, all of you. You're so brilliant, so clever, you're the best writer of our day – Russia's only hope, so sincere and natural, with your spontaneity and healthy humour. You can put over the essence of a person or landscape with one stroke of the pen. Your characters are so alive one can't read you without being moved. Too much hero-worship, you think? Think I'm flattering you? Then look in my eyes, come on. Do I look like a liar? There you see, I'm the only one who appreciates you, I'm the only one who tells you the truth, my wonderful darling. You will come, won't you? You won't desert me, will you?

(Trigorin agrees to leave with her)

Now he's mine. (*Casually*). Actually, you can stay on if you want. I'll leave on my own and you can come later, in a week's time. What's the hurry, after all?

Trigorin:
No, we may as well go together.

Irina:
As you like. We'll go together if you say so.

THE SEAGULL ACT 3

(Masha is talking to Boris Trigorin, a writer. She has always been in love with Constantin but her love is unrequited. She decides to marry Medvendenko, the schoolteacher instead. Masha drinks a little too much to dull her unhappiness).

<u>Masha:</u>
I'm telling you all this because you're a writer and can use it. Quite honestly, if he'd wounded himself seriously I couldn't have gone on living one minute. I'm quite brave, though, so I simply decided to wrench this love out of my heart and uproot it. By getting married. To Medvendenko.

To be hopelessly in love, just waiting, waiting for years on end -. But when I'm married I shan't bother about love, new worries will drive out old, and anyway it'll make a change, won't it? Shall we have another? (*she's referring to another drink*).

My schoolmaster's not all that bright, but he is kind. He's poor and very much in love with me. I'm sorry for him, and for his old mother too. Ah well, let me wish you all the best. Remember me kindly.

(*She shakes Trigorin's hand*).

Thanks for being so nice. Send me your books, and mind you write something in them, not 'with respects'. Just put: 'To Masha, who doesn't know where she comes from or what she's doing on this earth.' Good-bye.
(*She exits*)

Chekhov Scenes

THE SEAGULL ACT 4

(The scene takes place in Sorin's House. Nina has returned and makes her peace with Konstantin Trepliov)

Nina:
Lock the doors.

How warm, how nice it is here! … Have I changed a lot?
I was afraid that you might hate me. Every night I dream that you look at me and don't recognize me. Ever since I came I've been walking round here … beside the lake. I've been near this house many times, but I dared not come in.

Let us sit and talk …

Yesterday, late in the evening I came into the garden to see whether our stage was still there. And it is still standing! I began to cry for the first time in two years, and it lifted the weight from my heart, and I felt more at ease.

And so, you've become a writer … You are a writer and I'm an actress. I used to live here joyously, like a child – I used to wake up in the morning and burst into song. I loved you and dreamed of fame … And now? Tomorrow morning early I have to go to Yelietz in a third-class carriage … with the peasants; and at Yelietz, upstart business men will pester me with their attentions.

Life is coarse!

I've accepted an engagement for the whole winter. It's time to go. Don't see me off, I'll go by myself.

Why did you say you kissed the ground where I walked?
I am so tired. Oh, I wish I could rest … just rest! I'm a seagull …No, that's not it. I'm an actress.

(*She hears Trigorin laughing off stage*) So he is here, too! …

He didn't believe in the theatre, he was always laughing at my dreams, and so gradually I ceased to believe, too, and lost heart … And then I was so preoccupied with love and jealousy, and a constant fear for my baby … I became petty and common, when I acted I did it stupidly … I didn't know what to do with my hands or how to stand on the stage, I couldn't control my voice … But you can't imagine what it feels like – when you know that you are acting abominably.

…. Do you remember you shot a seagull? A man came along by chance, saw it and destroyed it, just to pass the time …
What was I talking about? …Yes, about the stage. I'm not like that now … Now I am a real actress, I act with intense enjoyment, with enthusiasm; on the stage I am intoxicated and I feel that I am beautiful. But now, while I'm living here, I go for walks a lot … I keep walking and thinking … thinking and feeling that I am growing stronger in spirit with every day that passes … I think I now, that what matters in our work – whether you act on the stage or write stories – what really matters is not fame, or glamour, not the things I used to dream about – but knowing how to endure things. How to bear one's cross and have faith. I have faith now and I'm not suffering quite so much, and when I think of my vocation, I'm not afraid of life.

Chekhov Scenes

UNCLE VANYA

This play follows the story of an elderly professor, Alexander Serebryakov, and his wife, Yelena. The setting is a country estate. Two men, Vanya and Astrov are visiting the estate. In fact, they are old friends and spend much of their time there. Vanya is the professor's late wife's brother. The professor spends a lot of time in the city with his new, much younger wife, Yelena, and it feels like a bit of an inconvenience when they return. Both Vanya and Astrov are a little in love with the professor's beautiful new wife, Yelena. The professor has a daughter named, Sonya, from his previous marriage. She has always helped her father manage the estate but her father, the professor, has decided to put it up for sale in order to finance his new lifestyle. By the end of Act 1, Vanya, realising Yelena is not fulfilled by her older husband, declares his love for her. Sonya, meanwhile, is in love with Astrov, the doctor, who has been called to the estate to aid the ailing Serebryakov. Astrov is not really aware of Sonya's feelings for him and is not in love with her. There has been some antagonism between Sonya and her stepmother in the past and both try to resolve their issues and develop a friendship in Act 2. Yelena reveals her marital unhappiness but she assures Sonya that she initially married for love. Sonya confesses her true feelings for the doctor, Astrov. Yelena, asks Dr Astrov if he has feelings for Sonya and after saying he doesn't, tries to kiss Yelena. Vanya witnesses this. Vanya argues with Serebryakov about his decision to sell the estate, leaving those who have worked tirelessly on it for years, with nowhere to go. Vanya attempts to shoot Serebryakov, but misses. Astrov decides to leave but on packing up, discovers that he is missing a bottle of morphine which Vanya has stolen. Sonya insists that Vanya returns it. The professor and his wife, Yelena, are still intending on leaving but agree that Vanya and the rest of the estate can remain in place with Vanya promising to send them money from the earnings from the estate. No one is really content.

Chekhov Scenes

UNCLE VANYA ACT 1

(Yeliena, is the second wife of an older husband, professor Alexander Serebryakov. Yeliena is talking to Astrov, a young doctor. She is becoming attracted to him).

Yeliena:
I've already heard how fond you are of forestry work. You can do a lot of good that way of course, but doesn't it interfere with your real business in life? You are a doctor after all.

You're still young, you don't look more than – well, thirty-six or seven – and you can't really find it as interesting as all that. Nothing but trees and more trees. It must be a bit monotonous, I should think.

(Astrov leaves the room, leaving Vanya Voynitsky with Yeliena. He is in love with her and accuses her of being bored)

I'm so bored too. They all run down my husband and look at me as if they're sorry for me. 'Poor girl, she's married to an old man'. This sympathy for me, oh how well I understand it. It's just what Astrov was saying a moment ago – you all wantonly destroy the forests, and so there won't be anything left on earth. You destroy men and women too every bit as wantonly, and soon, thanks to you, there will be no loyalty, integrity or unselfishness left on earth. Why does it upset you so much to see a woman who doesn't belong to you? Because – and the doctor's right – there's a demon of destruction in every one of you. You don't spare anything, whether it's the trees, the birds – or women or one another.

The doctor looks tired and highly strung. It's an attractive face. Sonya's obviously taken with him – she's in love with him, and I can understand that. He's been here three times since I arrived, but I'm rather shy, so we've never had a proper talk and I've never been really friendly to him. He doesn't think I'm very nice. Do you know why you and I are such good friends, Vanya? It must be because we're both such abysmal bores. Yes, bores! Don't look at me in that way, I don't like it.

Chekhov Scenes

UNCLE VANYA ACT 2

(Sonya is talking to Astrov, the doctor. She is in love with him but he seems unaware of the fact.)

Sonya:
Aren't you satisfied with life then?

You're not fond of anyone at all then?

Please don't drink any more.

You're so distinguished, you have such a gentle voice. And then again, you're so different from everyone else I know. You're a really fine man. So why ever should you want to be like ordinary people, the sort who drink and play cards? Oh, don't be like that. Please! You're always saying that man doesn't create anything, that he only destroys what God has given him. Then why, oh why, destroy your own self? Don't do it, don't do it, I beg you, I implore you.

Tell me, Dr Astrov, suppose I had a friend or a younger sister and you found out that she – well, let's say she loved you. What would be your attitude?

(Astrov exits)
(Sonya is left alone)

I told my uncle, 'You're so distinguished, such a fine man, you have such a gentle voice'. Surely that didn't sound out of place. His voice vibrates so tenderly, I can still hear it ringing in the air. But when I spoke about a younger sister he didn't understand. *(wringing her hands)*. Oh, how dreadful not to be beautiful. It's dreadful. And I know I'm not beautiful, I know, I know. Coming out of church last Sunday I heard some people talking about me and one woman said, 'She's such a nice, kind girl. What a pity she's so plain.' So plain.

Chekhov Scenes

UNCLE VANYA ACT 2

(Sonya is in love with the doctor, Astrov. Yeliena is talking to Sonya about their past differences.)

Yeliena:
The storm's over. What wonderful air.
When are you going to stop sulking? We've done each other no harm, so why should we be enemies? Can't we call it off?

Father's in the drawing-room. We don't speak to each other for weeks on end and heaven knows why.

Let's drink to our friendship. From the same glass. So we're friends now, Sonya?

But why are you crying? (*Yeliena starts to cry*). You silly girl, now I'm crying too.

You're angry with me because you think I married your father for selfish reasons. I give you my word of honour, if that means anything to you, that I married him for love. He attracted me as a scholar and public figure. It wasn't real love, it was quite artificial, but it seemed real enough at the time. It wasn't my fault. But since the day we were married you've been tormenting me by looking as if you knew what I was up to and didn't much like it.

You shouldn't look at people like that, it doesn't suit you. One must trust people or life becomes impossible.

Am I happy? No. What a child you are. Of course, I wish I was married to someone younger. And do I like the doctor? Yes, I do, very much.

He's a brilliant man. And you know what that means. It means he has courage, flair, tremendous vision. When he plants a tree he's already working out what the result will be in a thousand years' time, already glimpsing man's future happiness. People like that are rare and should be cherished. He drinks and is sometimes a bit rude, but never mind that. In Russia a brilliant man can't exactly be a saint. Just think what the doctor's life is like. Roads deep in mud, freezing cold, blizzards, enormous distances, coarse, brutal peasants, poverty and sickness on all sides. If a man does his job and battles on day in and day out in conditions like these, you can't expect that at the age of forty he'll still be a good little boy who doesn't drink. I wish you happiness with all my heart. You deserve it. As for me, I'm just a tiresome character and not a very important one. In my music, in my husband's house, in all my romantic affairs – in everything, that is – I've always played a minor role. Come to think of it, Sonya, I'm really very, very unhappy. There's no happiness for me in this world. None at all.

I feel like playing the piano. I'd like to play something now.
Just a minute, your father's still awake. Music annoys him when he's unwell. Go and ask him and I'll play something if he doesn't mind. Go on.

(Sonya exits)

It's ages since I played anything. I'll play and cry, cry my eyes out like a silly girl.

UNCLE VANYA ACT 3

(Yeliena, is the second wife of an older husband, professor Alexander Serebryakov. In Act 3, Yeliena's step daughter has announced that she is in love with Astrov. Yeliena is attracted to Astrov herself)

Yeliena:
Does Astrov know?

He's a strange man. I tell you what, let me talk to him. I'll be most discreet. I'll only drop a hint or two. Really, how much longer is this uncertainty to go on?

It won't be hard to find out whether he loves you or not. Now don't be embarrassed, my dear, don't worry, I'll question him so carefully he won't even notice. We only need to find out whether it's a yes or no. If it's a no he'd better stop coming here, don't you think?

It'll be easier for you if you don't see him. Now we won't keep putting it off, we'll question him straight away. He was going to show me some maps. You go and tell him I want to see him.

It's always better to know the truth, however bad, or that's what I think. Better than not knowing, anyway. Depend on me, dear.

(Sonya exits)

There's nothing worse than knowing someone else's secret and not being able to help. He's not in love with her, that's obvious, but why shouldn't he marry her? She isn't beautiful, but for a country doctor at his time of life she'd make an excellent wife. She's such a clever girl, so kind and unspoilt. But no, that's not really the point at all. I understand the poor child so well. In the middle of all this ghastly boredom, where there are no real people, but just dim, grey shapes drifting round, where you hear nothing but vulgar trivialities, where no one does anything but eat, drink and sleep – *he* appears from time to time, so different from the others, so handsome, charming and fascinating, like a bright moon rising in the darkness. To fall under the spell of such a man, to forget everything – I do believe I'm a little attracted myself. Yes, I'm bored when he's not about and here I am smiling as I think of him. And Uncle Vanya says I've mermaid's blood in my veins. 'Let yourself go for once in your life.' Well, and why not? Perhaps that would be the thing. Oh, to fly away, free as a bird, away from you all, away from your sleepy faces and your talk, to forget that you so much as exist! But I'm such a coward, I'm so shy. My conscience would torment me. He comes here every day now. I can guess why, and I already feel guilty. I want to kneel down and cry and ask Sonya to forgive me.

UNCLE VANYA ACT 3

(Sonya is talking to Yeliena about her love for the doctor, Astrov)

Sonya:
I'm glad Uncle went out, I must talk to you.

I'm not beautiful. No.

When a woman isn't beautiful, people always say, 'You have lovely eyes, you have lovely hair.' I've loved him for six years. I love him more than I loved my own mother. Every moment I seem to hear his voice or feel his hand in mine. I keep looking at the door, expecting him, thinking he's just going to come in and now, as you see, I'm always coming to you to talk about him. He visits us every day now, but he doesn't look at me, doesn't even see me. It's breaking my heart. There's no hope for me, no hope at all. (*Desperately*). God, give me strength. I spent the whole night praying. I often go up to him, start talking to him, look into his eyes. I've no pride left, no self-control. Yesterday I couldn't help telling Uncle Vanya I was in love, and all the servants know. Everyone knows.

He doesn't even notice me.

UNCLE VANYA ACT 4

(Written in 1897. The play takes place on the Serebryakov estate. This is the final scene of the play. Vanya Voynitsky and Sonya are alone. Voynitsky tells Sonya he is so depressed. Telegin quietly plays the guitar in the background).

<u>Sonya:</u>
Life must go on. And our life will go on, Uncle Vanya. We shall live through a long succession of days and endless evenings. We shall bear patiently the trials fate has in store for us. We shall work for others – now and in our old age – never knowing any peace. And when our time comes we shall die without complaining. In the world beyond the grave we shall say that we wept and suffered, that our lot was harsh and bitter, and God will have pity on us. And you and I, Uncle dear, shall behold a life which is bright and beautiful and splendid. We shall rejoice and look back on our present misfortunes with feelings of tenderness, with a smile. And we shall find peace. We shall, Uncle, I believe it with all my heart and soul. We shall find peace.
We shall hear the angels, we shall see the sky sparkling with diamonds. We shall see all the evils of this life, all our own sufferings, vanish in the flood of mercy which will fill the whole world. And then our life will be calm and gentle, sweet as a caress. I believe that, I do believe it. Poor, poor Uncle Vanya, you're crying. *(She hands him a handkerchief).* There's been no happiness in your life, but wait, Uncle Vanya, wait. We shall find peace. We shall find peace. We shall find peace.

THREE SISTERS

The play starts with three sisters, Olga, Masha and Irina and their brother, Andrei. They form the Prozorov family. The Prozorov's are an educated family from Moscow whose father was a General. He brought them to live in a small provincial town 11 years ago and the girls have missed living in Moscow ever since. Olga teaches at the local high school. Masha is married unhappily to Kulygin. She is bored with him and falls in love with Vershinin, a visiting army office who is also trapped in an unhappy marriage. Irina, the youngest sister, is courted by two officers, Solyony and Tuzenbach. Andrei has become a clerk at the Town Hall despite initially having aspirations to become a professor. He marries a dominating woman called Natasha and they have two children. The three sisters do not care for Natasha's vulgarity. Natasha gradually dominates the household. She takes the best rooms from her sisters in law and is rude to the servants. Irina chooses Tuzenbach over Solyony but is not in love with either of them. Solyony challenges Tuzenbach to a duel over this and Tuzenbach is killed. During Act Three there is a fire which affects the whole community. Andrei has started to gamble and incurs huge debts against the family home. Irina decides to leave town with the intention of becoming a school teacher. Olga becomes Headmistress of her school. Masha is forced to end her relationship with Vershinin as the army has to leave the region. The sisters never fulfil their dream of returning to Moscow.

Chekov Scenes

Chekov Scenes

THREE SISTERS ACT 1

(This is the opening scene of the play. Olga is reminiscing about the past and the fact that her father died exactly one year ago)

Olga:
It's been exactly one year since Father died – on your name day, Irina. It was bitter cold, snowing, remember? I didn't think I'd ever get through it. And you, you fainted dead away. But now a year has passed and it's easier to talk about. And you are wearing white again and you look radiant. (*She listens as the clock strikes*). The clock was striking then too. Remember, how the band was playing when they took father to the cemetery, how they fired a graveside salute? Hardly anyone came to the funeral and here he was a general, the commander of the brigade. Of course, it was raining and snowing heavily at the time. It's so warm we can have the windows open and yet there is not a single bud on the birch trees. Eleven years ago, when father was given command of the brigade, we all came here from Moscow. I can remember perfectly the beginning of May in Moscow. By this time in Moscow everything's in full bloom, and it's warm – everything is bathed in sunlight. Eleven years have passed. But I remember everything as if we'd left yesterday. Oh, dear God! When I woke up this morning and saw the sunlight everywhere, I knew right away it was spring time, and I felt my heart would burst with joy! I wanted so much to go home again. (*She hears Masha whistling*). Don't whistle Masha. How can you? (*Pause*) After teaching High School all day and then giving private lessons till dinner, I have a constant headache. And my thoughts – I've even started thinking like an old woman. In fact, for the past four years I've worked at the High School, every day I've felt my strength, my youth being drained off drop by drop. Only one thing, one dream keeps me strong, keeps me going ... Moscow!

Chekhov Scenes

THREE SISTERS ACT 1

(Irina is talking to the Doctor. It is her birthday and she is dressed all in white).

Irina:
Doctor, Doctor, dearest Doctor!

Tell me, why am I so happy today? I feel as if I was sailing along with a great blue sky above me and huge white birds soaring about. Tell me, why?

Today, I woke up, got out of bed and had a wash. And then I suddenly felt as if everything in the world made sense, I seemed to know how to live. I knew everything in the world made sense, I seemed to know how to live. I know everything, dearest Doctor. Man should work and toil by the sweat of his brow, whoever he is – that's the whole purpose and meaning of his life, his happiness and his joy.

How wonderful to be a workman who gets up at dawn and breaks stones in the road, or a shepherd, or a schoolmaster who teaches children or an engine-driver. Heavens, better not be a human being at all – better be an ox or just a horse, so long as you can work, rather than the kind of young woman who wakes up at noon, has her coffee in bed and then spends two hours getting dressed. Oh, that's so awful. You know how you sometimes long for a drink on a hot day – well that's how I long to work. And if I don't start getting up early and working you must stop being my friend, Doctor.

You're so used to seeing me as a little girl, you think it's funny when I look serious. I am twenty, you know.

Chekhov Scenes

THREE SISTERS ACT 2

(Irina continues to feel bored and weary. She is talking to her sister, Masha. It is clear that finances are low and her brother, Andrei, has gambling debts)

<u>Irina:</u>
Must have a rest. I'm so tired. I'm tired. Oh dear, I don't like working at the post office. I really don't. I must find another job. This one doesn't suit me. The things I'd hoped for and wanted so much – they're just what it doesn't give me. It's sheer drudgery with nothing romantic or intellectual about it. (*There is a knock on the floor from below*). That's the doctor banging.

(To Tuzenbach). Would you give him a knock, Nicholas? I can't, I'm too tired. He'll be up here in a moment. Something ought to be done about this business. The doctor went to the club with Andrew yesterday and they lost again. I heard Andrei was two hundred roubles down. He lost money a fortnight ago and also in December. The sooner he loses the lot the better, it might mean we'd leave this place. My God, do you know, I dream about Moscow every night? I feel as if I'd gone out of my mind. (*She laughs*). We're moving there in June, but it's, let me see – February, March, April, May – almost six months till June.

Natasha mustn't find out about his gambling. He hasn't paid his rent. We haven't had a thing from him for eight months. He's obviously forgotten.

Chekhov Scenes

THREE SISTERS ACT 2

(Natasha, Andrei's wife and sister in law to Olga, Masha and Irina, lives with her husband in the Prozorov household. In this scene she enters the dressing room around 8pm in the evening, wearing a dressing gown and carrying a candle. She is talking to her husband, Andrei. She is a crafty, manipulative woman who is trying to usurp the three sister's authority by ensuring her own children take precedence. Her son is called Bobik and she fusses terribly over him).

Natasha:
What are you doing, Andrei? Reading, are you? It's all right. I only wondered. I thought someone might have left a light burning. I was seeing if there were any lights on. It's carnival week and the servants are in such a state anything might happen – you need eyes in the back of your head. Last night I went through the dining-room about midnight and found a candle burning. But who lit it? That's what I couldn't find out. (*She puts down her candle*). What time is it?

Olga and Irina aren't here yet. They're still not back from work, poor things. Olga's at a staff meeting and Irina's at the post office. I was telling that sister of yours only this morning. 'You look after yourself, Irina dear,' I said. But she won't listen. A quarter past eight, you say? I'm afraid little Bobik isn't at all well. Why does he get so chilly? Yesterday he had a temperature and today he's cold all over. I'm so worried. He'd better be on a special diet. I'm so worried. And I'm told there are some people calling here about half past nine, a fancy dress party from the carnival. I'd much rather they didn't come, dear.

The sweet little thing woke up this morning and looked at me, and suddenly he smiled. He knew who I was, you see. 'Good morning, Bobik,' I said. 'Good morning, darling.' And he laughed. Babies do understand, oh yes, they understand very well. All right then, dear, I'll say those carnival people aren't to be asked in.

Yes, I know it's your sisters house too. I'll have a word with them, they're so kind. (*She moves to go*). I've ordered some yogurt for supper. The doctor says you shouldn't eat anything but yogurt or you'll never lose weight. (*She stops*). Bobik gets so chilly. I'm afraid his room may be too cold. We ought to put him somewhere else, at least till the weather's warmer. Irina's room, for instance, is just right for a baby, it's not damp and it gets the sun all day. We must have a word with her, she can go in with Olga for the time being. She's never at home during the day anyway, she only sleeps here. (*Pause*) Andrew, sweetie-pie, why don't you say something?

Chekhov Scenes

THREE SISTERS ACT 3

(Irina is feeling depressed and feels she will never get to Moscow or meet the man of her dreams).

Irina:
It's true, how small minded our Andrei has become. How he's wasted himself and grown old, living with that woman! There was a time when he was aiming to be a professor, but now, only yesterday he was boasting that he's at last managed to be elected as a member of the local district council. He's a member of the council, and Protopopov is chairman … the whole town is talking about it and laughing at him, but he is the only one who knows nothing and sees nothing … Just now everyone ran to help to fight the fire, but he sat alone in his study and did not give it a thought. He just plays on the violin. It's terrible, terrible, terrible! *(She cries)* It's too much for me, I can't bear it any longer! … I can't, I can't …. *(She sobs bitterly).*

Don't have anything more to do with me, don't, don't, I can't bear it any longer! *(Sobbing).* Where? Where has it all gone? Where is it? Oh my God, my God! I have forgotten everything, forgotten everything … Everything is confused in my head … I can't remember what is the word for window in Italian, for ceiling … I am forgetting everything. I forget more every day, and life flies past and never returns, never, and we will never go to Moscow … I see now that we will never go …. *(gaining some control).* Oh, I'm so unhappy … I can't work, I won't work. That's enough! That's enough! I worked in the Telegraph Office, now I am employed by the Town Council, and I hate and despise everything that they give me to do …

I'm already twenty four, I have been working already for ages, my brain is drying up, I'm growing ugly and old, and nothing I do, nothing at all gives me any joy, and time goes flying by and all the time it seems as if you are abandoning real life, life that is beautiful, you are going farther and farther away from it, over some sort of precipice. I am in total despair, and how I am alive, why I have not killed myself before now I do not understand… I won't cry, I won't cry… That's enough! …Look, I've already

Chekhov Scenes

stopped crying. That's enough… that's enough! I kept on waiting, thinking we would settle in Moscow, and there my ideal man would meet me, I dreamed about him, I love him …But it turns out it was all nonsense, all nonsense ….

Chekhov Scenes

THREE SISTERS ACT 3

(Natasha is talking to Olga, her sister in law, about the old servant, Anfisa. She feels she is past her usefulness and wants her to return to her village).

<u>Natasha:</u>
They're saying we ought to set up a relief committee at once for the fire victims. You know, that's not a bad idea. In fact, we should always be ready to help the poor. It's up to the rich, isn't it? Bobik and little Sophie are sound asleep in bed just as if nothing had happened. There's such a crowd in the house, with people everywhere whichever way you turn. And now there's flu about in town I'm afraid the children might catch it.

People say I've put on weight. But it's not true, not a bit of it. Masha's asleep – tired out, poor girl.

(She sees the old maid, Anfisa sitting down and turns abruptly on her)

How dare you be seated in my presence? Stand up! Be off with you*! (Anfisa leaves).* Why you keep that old woman I don't understand. There's no place for her here. She came from a village and she should go back to her village. This is sheer extravagance. I like to see a house run properly, there's no room for misfits in this house. *(Natasha strokes Olga's cheeks).* Poor thing, you're tired out. Our headmistress is tired. You know, when little Sophie grows up and goes to school, I'll be quite scared of you. But they're appointing you Headmistress, dear, it's all settled.

Forgive me, Olga. I didn't mean to upset you. I often say the wrong thing, I admit, but you must agree, dear, she could go and live in her village. The point is she can't work anymore. Either I don't understand you or you've made up your mind not to understand me. She can't do a proper job, all she does is sleep or sit around.

Let her sit around! She's a servant, isn't she? I can't make you out, Olga. I keep a nanny myself and a wet nurse for the baby, and we have a maid and a cook. But what do we need that old woman for? That's what I don't see.

We must get this straight once and for all, Olga. Your place is the school, mine is the home. You teach. I run the house. And if I happen to pass a remark about the servants I know what I'm talking about. And the sooner you get that into your head the better. So you mind that thieving old hag gets her marching orders for tomorrow. The old bitch! How dare you exasperate me like this, how dare you. (*regaining her self-control*). Really, if you don't move downstairs we'll never stop quarrelling. It's perfectly horrible.

Chekhov Scenes

THREE SISTERS ACT 3

(Masha confesses to her sisters that she is in love with Vershinin)

Masha:
My dears, I've a confession to make. I feel I must get it off my chest. I'll tell you right away. (*quietly*) It's my secret, but I want you to know it, I can't keep it to myself. (*Pause*) I'm in love, in love with that man. He was in here just now. Oh, what's the use? What I'm saying is, I love Vershinin.

It's hopeless. I found him strange at first, then felt sorry for him, then fell in love with him – with him, with his voice, his conservation, his misfortunes and his two little girls.

Since I love him it must be my fate, it must be my destiny. And he loves me. It's terrifying, isn't it? Isn't it? (*She draws Irina towards her*). Oh darling, how shall we spend the rest of our lives, and what's to become of us? When you read a novel this sort of thing all seems so trite and obvious, but when you fall in love yourself you see that nobody knows anything and we all have to decide these things for ourselves. My dears, now I've confessed I'll say no more. Now I'll be like the madman in Gogol's story. I'll keep quiet and say nothing.

Chekov Scenes

THE CHERRY ORCHARD

The play is set in the cherry orchard estate. Madame Ranevsky, owns the estate but has been away living in Paris for the past five years. She has two daughters, Anya and Varya. Her husband and young son are dead. Madame Ranevsky has been living with an abusive lover in Paris who has taken advantage of her money and she is now almost penniless. The play takes place during the revolution when Russian peasants were fighting for liberation. A local businessman and former serf named Lopakhin has become extremely wealthy during this period. Madame Ranevsky can no longer afford to pay the mortgage on her estate and discussions ensue about having to sell the cherry orchard. Lopakhin suggests that perhaps they could build villas on the estate and rent them out. Madame Ranevsky and her brother, Gayef, are opposed to this idea. Trofimov, an insightful student, is in love with Anya. Dunyasha and Yasha, two servants, also have a romantic relationship. There is an auction for the cherry orchard estate. On the same evening, Madame Ranevsky holds a ball. She seems to have no consideration of the extravagance or cost of this. She continues to increase her debts and also considers returning to Paris to be reunited with her abusive partner. She does not seem to be in touch with reality. When her brother, Gayef and the businessman, Lopakhin, return from town, they discover that it is Lopakhin who has purchased the estate. The family are shocked at Lopakhin's achievement and excitement regarding it. He has managed to buy the estate where his family had formally been slaves. The family will now have to vacate the cherry orchard estate. As they leave, they hear the sound of axes cutting down their beloved orchard.

Chekov Scenes

Chekov Scenes

THE CHERRY ORCHARD ACT 1

(Anya has recently returned from France. Their money has been running out. The Cherry Orchard has been put up for sale).

Anya:
I've had a terrible time.

I left just before Easter and it was cold then. On the way there Charlotte kept talking and doing those awful tricks of hers. Why you ever landed me with Charlotte – It was cold and snowing when we got to Paris. My French is atrocious. I find Mother living on the fourth floor somewhere and when I got there she had visitors, French people – some ladies and an old priest with a little book. The place is full of smoke and awfully uncomfortable. Suddenly I felt sorry for Mother, so sorry, I took her head in my arms and held her and just couldn't let go. Afterwards Mother was terribly sweet to me and kept crying. She's already sold her villa near Menton and had nothing left, nothing at all. I hadn't any money either, there was hardly enough for the journey. And Mother simply won't understand. If we have a meal in a station restaurant she asks for all the most expensive things and tips the waiters a rouble each. And Charlotte's no better. Then Yasha wants to have his share as well, it was simply awful. Mother has this servant Yasha, you know, we've brought him with us –

Have you paid the interest?

My God, how dreadful! This estate is up for sale in August. Oh my God!

Someone ought to let Mother know that Peter's here.

It's six years since Father died. And a month after that our brother Grisha was drowned in the river. He was a lovely little boy, only seven years old. It was too much for mother, she went away, just dropped everything and went. (*She shudders*). How well I understand her, if only she knew. (*Pause*), Peter Trofimov was Grisha's tutor, he might bring back memories.

THE CHERRY ORCHARD ACT 2

(Mrs Ranevsky reminisces about her marriage, her time in France, and the death of her young son)

Mrs Ranevsky:
Oh, my sins. Look at the mad way I've always wasted money, spent it like water, and I married a man who could do nothing but run up debts. My husband died of champagne, he drank like a fish, and then I had the bad luck to fall in love with someone else and have an affair with him. And just then came my first punishment, and what a cruel blow that was! In the river here – My little boy was drowned and I went abroad, went right away, never meaning to return or see the river again. I shut my eyes and ran away, not knowing what I was doing, and *he* followed me. It was a cruel, brutal thing to do. I bought a villa near Menton because he fell ill there and for three years, I had no rest, nursing him day and night. He utterly wore me out. All my feelings seemed to have dried up inside me. Then last year, when the villa had to be sold to pay my debts, I left for Paris where he robbed me, deserted me and took up with another woman. I tried to poison myself. It was all so stupid and humiliating. Then I suddenly longed to be back in Russia, back in my own country with my little girl. (*She dries her eyes*). Lord, Lord, be merciful, forgive me my sins. Don't punish me anymore. (*She takes a telegram from her pocket*). This came from Paris today. He asks my forgiveness and begs me to go back. (*She tears up the telegram*).

THE CHERRY ORCHARD ACT 3

(Mrs Ranvesky is talking to Peter Trofimov about the sale of the Cherry Orchard estate. Mrs Ranevsky loves Peter like her own son and is happy to confide her feelings to him)

Mrs Ranevsky:
If only I knew whether the estate's been sold or not. I feel that such an awful thing just couldn't happen, so I don't know what to think, I'm at my wits' end. I'm liable to scream or do something silly. Help me, Peter. Oh, say something, do, for heaven's sake speak.

What truth? *You* can see what's true or untrue, but I seem to have lost my sight, I see nothing. You solve the most serious problems so confidently, but tell me, dear boy, isn't that because you're young – not old enough for any of your problems to have caused you real suffering? You face the future so bravely, but then you can't imagine anything terrible happening, can you? And isn't that because you're still too young to see what life's really like? You're bolder, more honest, more profound than we are, but try and put yourself in our place, do show a little generosity and spare my feelings. You see, I was born here, my father and mother lived here, and my grandfather too. I love this house. Without the cherry orchard life has no meaning for me and if it really must be sold then you'd better sell me with it. (*She hugs Trofimov and kisses him*)

My little boy was drowned here, you know. (*She weeps*). Don't be too hard on me, my good kind friend.

I'm so depressed today, you just can't imagine. I hate all this noise. Every sound sends a shiver right through me. I'm trembling all over, but I can't go to my room, the silence frightens me when I'm on my own. Don't think too badly of me, Peter. I love you as my own son. I'd gladly let Anya marry you, I honestly would, only you really must study, dear boy, you must take your degree. You never do anything, you just drift about from place to place, that's what's so peculiar. Well, it is, isn't it? And you should do something about that beard, make it grow somehow. (*She laughs*)

Chekhov Scenes

You do look funny.

That telegram's from Paris. I get one every day. One came yesterday and there's another today. That crazy creature is ill and in trouble again. He asks my forgiveness, begs me to come to him, and I really ought to go over to Paris and be near him for a bit. You look very disapproving, Peter, but what else can I do, my dear boy, what else can I do? He's ill, he's lonely and unhappy, and who'll look after him there? Who'll stop him making a fool of himself and give him his medicine at the right time? And then, why make a secret of it, why not say so? I love him, that's obvious. I love him, I love him. He's a millstone round my neck and he's dragging me down with him, but I love my millstone and I can't live without it. *(She takes Trofimov's hand).* Don't think badly of me, Peter, and don't say anything, don't talk.

You're twenty-six or twenty-seven, but you're still a schoolboy. You should be more of a man. At your age you should understand people in love. And you should be in love yourself, you should fall in love. *(Angrily).* Yes, I mean it. And you're not all that pure and innocent either, you're just a prig, a ridiculous freak, a kind of monster – 'I am above love!' You're not above love, you're just what our friend Firs calls a nincompoop. Fancy being your age and not having a mistress!

MY LIFE CHAPTER 19

My Life is a novella about a man who is so disillusioned with aristocratic life that he decides to live his life among the working class.

The sister, Cleopatra, is talking to her brother, Misail, about a young woman named Anuita Blagovo who is in love with him.

Sister:
When you wanted to get away from the office and become a house-painter, Aniuta Blagovo and I knew from the very beginning that you were right, but we were afraid to say so. Tell me, what power is it that keeps us from saying what we feel? There's Aniuta Blagovo. She loves you, adores you, and she knows that you are right. She loves me, too, like a sister, and she knows that I am right, and in her heart she envies me, but some power prevents her coming to see us. She avoids us. She is afraid.

If you only knew how she loves you! She confessed it to me and to no one else, very hesitatingly, in the dark. She used to take me out into the garden, into the dark, and begin to tell me in a whisper how dear you were to her. You will see that she will never marry because she loves you. Are you sorry for her?

(Her brother says that he is sorry for her)

It was she sent the bread. She is funny. Why should she hide herself? I used to be silly and stupid, but I left all that and I am not afraid of any one, and I think and say aloud what I like – and I am happy. When I lived at home I had no notion of happiness, and now I would not change places with a queen.

Chekhov Scenes

MY LIFE CHAPTER 19

This is Masha's letter.

Masha:
'My dear, kind M.A.,
My brave, sweet angel, as the old painter calls you, good-bye. I am going to America with my father for the exhibition. In a few days I shall be on the ocean – so far from Dubechnia. It is awful to think of! It is vast and open like the sky and I long for it and freedom. I rejoice and dance about and you see how incoherent my letter is. My dear Misail, give me my freedom. Quick, snap the thread which still holds and binds us. My meeting and knowing you was a ray from heaven, which brightened my existence. But, you know, my becoming your wife was a mistake, and the knowledge of the mistake weighs me down, and I implore you on my knees, my dear, generous friend, quick – quick – before I go over the sea – wire that you will agree to correct our mutual mistake, remove then the only burden on my wings, and my father who will be responsible for the whole business, has promised me not to overwhelm you with formalities. So, then, I am free of the whole world? Yes?

Be happy. God bless you. Forgive my wickedness. I am alive and well. I am squandering money on all sorts of follies, and every minute I thank God that such a wicked woman as I am has no children. I am singing and I am a success, but it is not a passing whim. No. It is my haven, my convent cell where I go for rest. King David had a ring with an inscription: "Everything passes." When one is sad, these words make one cheerful; and when one is cheerful, they make one sad. And I have got a ring with the words written in Hebrew, and this talisman will keep me from losing my heart and head. Or does one need nothing but consciousness of freedom, because, when one is free, one wants nothing, nothing, nothing? Snap the thread then.

I embrace you and your sister warmly. Forgive and forget your M.'

Chekhov Scenes

A MARRIAGE PROPOSAL

(This play is from one of seven one-act farces written between 1886-1891. It is sometimes known as 'The Proposal'. 25yr old, Natalia Tschubukov is visited by her neighbour, 35 yr old Lomov. He is smartly dressed. As he is nervous, he does not make his motive clear at first. After an argument over some meadow land, Lomov eventually leaves their house. Mr Tschubukov informs his daughter of the proposal and a shocked, Natalia demands that her father calls him back to resolve the former disagreement and misunderstanding)

Natalia:
How do you do, Ivan Vassilevitch?

Excuse my apron, and not being dressed. We're shelling peas. Oh, do sit down.

The weather's nice today … Have you got much hay in?

But why are you so dressed up? Is there a dance or something?

I hate to interrupt you, but you said: 'MY Oxen Meadows'. Do you really think they're yours?

The Oxen Meadows are ours, not yours!

Now, come, Ivan Vassilevitch! How long have they been yours?

Both my grandfather and my great-grandfather said that their land went as far as the marsh, which means that the Meadows are ours! There's nothing whatever to argue about. Here we have had the land for hundreds of years, and suddenly you try to tell us it isn't ours. What's wrong with you? Those meadows aren't even fifteen acres, and they're not worth three hundred roubles, but I just can't stand unfairness!
It's just nonsense, this whole business about aunts and grandfathers and grandmothers. The Meadows are ours! That's all there is to it!

Chekhov Scenes

You can go on talking for two days, and you can put on fifteen evening coats and twenty pairs of gloves, but I tell you they're ours, ours, ours!

I'll give them to YOU! Because they're ours! And if I may say, your behaviour is very strange. Until now, we've always considered you a good neighbour, even a friend. And here you are treating us like a pack of gypsies. Giving me my own land, indeed! Really! Why that's not being a good neighbour. It's sheer impudence, that's what it is …

Please don't shout! You can shout all you want in your own house, but here I must ask you to control yourself.

Papa, send the mowers out to the meadows at once!

Your father was a rum-soaked gambler. Your aunt was queen of the scandalmongers! Don't ever set foot in our house again!

What a rascal! How can you trust your neighbours after an incident like that?

(Ivan Vassilevitch leaves. Natalie's father tells her that Ivan had come to propose to her)

What proposal?

To propose? To me? Why didn't you tell me before? To propose to me? Ohhhh! *(she falls into a chair and starts wailing).* Bring him back! Back! Go get him! Bring him back! *(wailing).*

You must forgive us, Ivan Vassilevitch. We all got too excited. I remember now. The Oxen Meadows are yours. Yes, the Meadows are all yours. Do sit down.

We were wrong, of course.

Chekhov Scenes

THE BRUTE – A ONE ACT FARCE

(This short one act farce is a romantic comedy. Mrs Popov is mourning her late husband. She has been left with her husband's debts and struggles to survive. Her neighbour, Mr Smirnov arrives one day insisting that she pays debts owed to him. Mrs Popov refuses and an argument ensues resulting in Mrs Popov reaching for her husband's pistols. Mr Smirnov is amused and impressed by her audacity. The humour is heightened due to the fact that Mrs Popov hasn't a clue how to use the pistols. Mr Smirnov is amused at her spirit and by the end of this short one-act play Mr Smirnov ends up falling in love with Mrs Popov. In this scene she is talking to her maid, Luka).

Mrs Popov:
I must never set foot out of doors again, Luka. Never! I have nothing to set foot out of doors for. My life is done. He is in his grave. I have buried myself alive in this house. Since Popov died, life has been an empty dream to me, you know that. YOU may think I am alive. Poor ignorant Luka! You are wrong. I am dead. I'm in my grave. Never more shall I see the light of day, never strip from my body this ... raiment of death! Are you listening, Luka? Let his ghost learn how I love him! Yes, I know, and you know, he was often unfair to me, he was cruel to me, and he was unfaithful to me. What of it? I shall be faithful to him, that's all. I will show him how I can love. Hereafter, in a better world that this, he will welcome me back, the same loyal girl I always was –

Toby! You said Toby! He adored that horse. When he drove me out to the Korchagins and the Vlasovs, it was always with Toby! He was a wonderful driver, you remember, Luka? So graceful! So strong! I can see him now, pulling at those reins with all his might and main! Toby! Luka, tell them to give Toby an extra portion of oats today.

(A bell rings)

Who is that? Tell them I'm not at home.

(gazing at her dead husband's photograph).

Chekhov Scenes

You shall see, Mr Popov, how a wife can love and forgive. Till death do us part. Longer than that. Till death re-unite us forever! Aren't you ashamed of yourself, Popov? Here's your little wife, being good, being faithful, so faithful she's locked up waiting for her own funeral, while you – doesn't it make you ashamed, you naughty boy? You were terrible, you know. You were unfaithful, and you made those awful scenes about it, you stormed out and left me alone for weeks –

I suppose you told him that since my husband's death, I see no one? In the dining room, is he? I'll give him his come uppance. Bring him in here this minute.

Why do they do this to me? Why? Insulting my grief, intruding on my solitude? I'm afraid I'll have to enter a convent. I will, I MUST enter a convent!

THE BRUTE – A ONE ACT FARCE

(This short one act farce is a romantic comedy. Mrs Popov is mourning her late husband. She has been left with her husband's debts and struggles to survive. Her neighbour, Mr Smirnov arrives one day insisting that she pays debts owed to him. Mrs Popov refuses and an argument ensues resulting in Mrs Popov reaching for her husband's pistols. Mr Smirnov is amused and impressed by her audacity. The humour is heightened due to the fact that Mrs Popov hasn't a clue how to use the pistols. Mr Smirnov is amused at her spirit and by the end of this short one-act play Mr Smirnov ends up falling in love with Mrs Popov)

Mrs Popov:
What is it you wish, sir?

Twelve hundred roubles? But what did my husband owe it to you for?

My dear Mr – what was the name again?

My dear Mr Smirnov, if Mr Popov owed you money, you shall be paid – to the last rouble, to the last kopeck. But today – you must excuse me, Mr. – what was it?

Today, Mr Smirnov, I have no ready cash in the house.

Tomorrow, Mr Smirnov, no, the day after tomorrow, all will be well. My steward will be back from town. I shall see that he pays what is owing ... Today, no. In any case, today is exactly seven months from Mr Popov's death. On such a day you will understand that I am in no mood to think of money.

Be sensible, Mr Smirnov. How can I pay you if I don't have it?

What language! What a tone to take to a lady! I refuse to hear another word.

In the solitude of my rural retreat, Mr Smirnov, I've long since grown unaccustomed to the sound of the human voice. Above all, I cannot bear shouting. I must beg you not to break the silence.

Not a rouble, not a kopeck. Get out! Leave me alone! I won't talk to you a moment longer.

You're a wild animal, you were never house-broken. Trying to scare me? Just because you have big fists and a voice like a bull? You're a brute. You want to shoot it out?

I'll have Popov's pistols here in one minute! Putting one of Popov's bullets through your silly head will be a pleasure!

(She fetches the pistols)

Pistols, Mr Smirnov! But before we start, you'd better show me how it's done, I'm not too familiar with these things. In fact, I never gave a pistol a second look.

This way?

(She has no idea how to hold a pistol)

I see.

And if it's inconvenient to do the job here, we can go out in the garden. My blood is up. I won't be happy till I've drilled a hole through that skull of yours.

THE ANNIVERSARY – A ONE ACT FARCE

(This comedy is from one of Chekhov's one act farces. Tatyana has returned from a trip to her home town and is eager to inform her husband of her adventures. Unfortunately, her husband, Mr Andrei Shipuchin, a Banker is preparing for a very important meeting with his shareholders to celebrate the 15th Anniversary at the bank. Despite loving his overzealous young wife, he is eager for her to leave for he has much to do before the evening's celebrations).

Tatyana:
Have you missed me? Oh, how are you, my darling? I haven't been home yet, I came straight from the station. I've so much to tell you, I couldn't wait. I won't take my coat off, though. I'll be off in a minute. Is all well at home? Good. Mother and Katya send their love. Valissy told me to give you a kiss, so here goes. Auntie sent a pot of her home-made jam and everyone's furious with you for not writing. Oh yes, Zina sends a kiss too. Oh darling, if you've any idea what's been going on, if you only knew! What a palava!

But you don't seem very pleased with me. Oh, of course, it's the Anniversary. Congratulations, darling. Congratulations, gentlemen. So today's the meeting and the dinner. Lovely. Remember that lovely address to the shareholder? The one that took you so long to write. Are they presenting that today?

Go home? Yes, of course, I'll go home. But I must tell you … I must tell you all about it. From the very beginning. After you saw me off on the train, I sat next to a fat woman, remember? And I started reading. Well, you know how much I hate talking on trains. I read for three whole stops and said not a word, not to anyone. Then it started to get dark and … well, it's always rather depressing when it gets dark, isn't it? There was a young man sitting opposite me, dark hair, quite good looking – terribly attractive, actually. We fell into a conversation. A sailor came along then some student or other. You'll never guess. I told them I was single and they were all over me. We talked and talked and talked – till long past midnight. The dark young man told screamingly funny stories and the sailor kept singing rather risqué songs! I laughed so much I thought I'd burst. And when the sailor – oh, those sailors! – when he found out I was called Tatyana, he kept singing bits from Eugene Onegin.

Sergei met me at the station. Then another young man turned up – a tax inspector, I think he said – and we all got chatting and we all went for a coffee together. The tax inspector had lovely eyes! And the weather! It was glorious.

What? You're busy? Oh dear, have I said the wrong thing?

Well, why didn't you say so?

THE ANNIVERSARY – A ONE ACT FARCE

(This comedy is from one of Chekhov's one act farces. Mr Andrei Shipuchin, a Banker is preparing for a very important meeting with his shareholders to celebrate the 15th Anniversary at the bank. He has much to do before the evening's celebrations. Mrs Merchutkina, an obsessed woman barges in to the office in a highly distressed state. Her husband is owed money from his work and, illogically, she expects the bank to pay her for his lost income. She refuses to leave and after paying her some money, in desperation, they chase her from the bank. It is at this moment, that the shareholders enter).

Mrs Merchutkin:
I want to see the manager!

Oh, your Honour, I have the honour … my name is Nastasia Merchutkin. My husband's in the civil service. Was.

Well, you see, your Honour, my husband was sick for five months, and while he was home, under the doctor's care, they discharged him from the civil service, for no reason whatsoever, your Honour. And when I went to collect his salary they took 24 roubles and 36 kopecks out of it, your Honour. 'What for?' I asked them. 'That's what he borrowed from the Mutual Aid fund', they said. What do they mean? Why should he borrow money without my consent? What sort of business is that, your Honour? I'm just a poor woman. I have to take in boarders to keep alive. I'm a poor, weak, defenceless woman, your Honour. Everybody insults me, and I don't get a kind word from anyone!

I've been to five other places already and no one will listen to me. It was driving me crazy till my son-in-law – Boris Matveytich, gave me the idea of coming to you. 'You go to Mr Shipuchin, mama', he said, 'He's a big man, he's got influence. He can do anything for you.' You've got to help me, your Honour.

I've got a doctor's certificate to prove my husband was sick. There it is!

Chekhov Scenes

Couldn't you at least make them pay me 15 roubles on account? I'm a weak, defenceless woman. I'm worn out and worried to death. My boarders are suing me, I've got this business on my hands, I have to run the house, and my son-on-law's out of a job! I may look strong, but if you gave me an operation you'd see that not one part of my body's normal. I can hardly stand on my feet, and I didn't even enjoy my coffee this morning. All I'm asking is: do I get what's coming to me or not? I'm not interested in anybody else's money, just mine.

When do I get the money? I need it right away. If the medical certificate isn't enough I'll get an affidavit from the police. Tell them to give me the money!

(In desperation, Shipuchin gives her 25 roubles and tells her to keep the change. He wants to get rid of her)

Oh, thank you kindly, your Honour.

What about my husband's job, your Honour? Can he have it back?

(Hirin and Shipuchin start chasing the mad woman around the room, shouting out, Get Out, Catch her! Cut her throat!))

Holy saints in heaven! Holy saints! (*squealing*) Holy saints alive!

Chekhov Scenes

DUOLOGUES

Chekhov Scenes

UNCLE VANYA ACT 2

(Sonya and Yeliena have a heart to heart and try to resolve their past differences).

Yeliena:
The storm's over. What wonderful air. (*Pause*) Where's the doctor?

Sonya:
Gone home.

Yeliena:
Sonya?

Sonya:
What?

Yeliena:
When are you going to stop sulking? We've done each other no harm, so why should we be enemies? Can't we call it off?

Sonya:
I've wanted to myself. (*She kisses her*). Let's not be angry any more.

Yeliena:
That's splendid. (*They are both touched*)

Sonya:
Has father gone to bed?

Yeliena:
No, he's in the drawing-room. We don't speak to each other for weeks on end and heaven knows why. Let's drink to our friendship.

Sonya:
Yes, let's.

Yeliena:
From the same glass. (*She fills a glass*). That's better. So, we're

friends now, Sonya?

Sonya:
Friends, Yeliena. (*They drink together and hug*). I've wanted to make it up for ages, but I felt too embarrassed somehow. *(She cries)*

Yeliena:
But why are you crying?

Sonya:
Never mind, it's nothing.

Yeliena:
There, there, that'll do. *(She cries)*. You silly girl, now I'm crying too. (*Pause*) You're angry with me because you think I married your father for selfish reasons. I give you my word of honour, if that means anything to you, that I married him for love. He attracted me as a scholar and public figure. It wasn't real love, it was quite artificial, but it seemed real enough at the time. It wasn't my fault. But since the day we were married you've been tormenting me by looking as if you knew what I was up to and didn't much like it.

Sonya:
Please, please, remember we're friends now. Let's forget all that.

Yeliena:
You shouldn't look at people like that, it doesn't suit you. One must trust people or life becomes impossible. *(Pause)*.

Sonya:
Tell me honestly, as a friend. Are you happy?

Yeliena:
No.

Sonya:
I knew it. Another question. Tell me frankly, do you wish you were married to somebody younger?

Yeliena:
What a child you are. Of course, I do. (*She laughs*) All right, ask me something else, go on.

Sonya:
Do you like the doctor?

Yeliena:
Yes, I do, very much.

Sonya:
I have a foolish expression on my face, haven't I? He's just left, but I can still hear his voice and footsteps. And if I look into a dark window I seem to see his face in it. Let me finish what I have to say. But I can't say it out loud like this, I feel too embarrassed. Let's go to my room and talk there. Do you think I'm silly? You do, don't you? Tell me something about him.

Yeliena:
Alright.

Sonya:
He's so intelligent. He can do anything, he's so clever. He practices medicine, plants trees –

Yeliena:
There's a bit more to it than medicine and trees. Don't you see, my dear? He's a brilliant man. And you know what that means? It means he has courage, flair, tremendous vision. When he plants a tree he's already working out what the result will be in a thousand years' time, already glimpsing man's future happiness. People like that are rare and should be cherished. He drinks and is sometimes a bit rude, but never mind that. In Russia, a brilliant man does his job and battles on day in day out in conditions like these, you can't expect that at the age of forty he'll still be a good little boy who doesn't drink. (*She kisses her*). I wish you happiness with all my heart. You deserve it. (*She stands up*). As for me, I'm just a tiresome character and not a very important one. In my music, in my husband's house, in all my romantic affairs – in everything, that is – I've always played a minor role. Come to think

of it, Sonya, I'm really very, very unhappy. (*She walks up and down in agitation*).
There is no happiness for me in this world. None at all. What are you laughing at?

Sonya:
I'm so happy. So happy.

Yeliena:
I feel like playing the piano. I'd like to play something now.

Sonya:
Yes, do. I can't sleep. Do play something.

Yeliena:
Just a minute, your father's still awake. Music annoys him when he's unwell. Go and ask him and I'll play something if he doesn't mind. Go on.

Sonya:
Alright.

Yeliena:
It's ages since I played anything. I'll play and cry, cry my eyes out like a silly girl.

THE CHERRY ORCHARD ACT 1

(Anya has recently arrived home from Paris with her mother, Madame Ranevsky. She catches up with her adopted sister, Varya).

<u>Varya:</u>
Well, thank heavens you're back. You're home again. My lovely darling, Anya's home again.

<u>Anya:</u>
I've had a terrible time.

<u>Varya:</u>
So I can imagine.

<u>Anya:</u>
I left just before Easter and it was cold then. On the way there Charlotte kept talking and doing those awful tricks of hers. Why you ever landed me with Charlotte …

<u>Varya:</u>
But you couldn't have gone on your own, darling. A girl of seventeen.

<u>Anya:</u>
It was cold and snowing when we got to Paris. My French is atrocious. I find Mother living on the fourth floor somewhere and when I get there she has visitors, French people – some ladies and an old priest with a little book. The place is full of smoke and awfully uncomfortable. Suddenly I felt sorry for Mother, so sorry, I took her head in my arms and held her and just couldn't let go. Afterwards, Mother was terribly sweet to me and kept crying.

<u>Varya:</u>
Don't, Anya. I can't bear it.

<u>Anya:</u>
She'd already sold her villa near Menton and had nothing left, nothing at all. I hadn't any money either, there was hardly enough

for the journey. And Mother simply won't understand. If we have a meal in a station restaurant she asks for all the most expensive things and tips the waiters a rouble each. And Charlotte's no better. Then Yasha has to have his share as well, it was simply awful. Mother has this servant, Yasha, you know, we've brought him with us …

Varya:
Yes, I've seen him. Isn't he foul?

Anya:
Well, how is everything? Have you paid the interest?

Varya:
What a hope.

Anya:
My God, how dreadful.

Varya:
This estate is up for sale in August.

Anya:
Oh my God!

Has Lopakhin proposed, Varya? But he does love you. Why can't you get it all settled? What are you both waiting for?

Varya:
I don't think anything will come of it. He's so busy he can't be bothered with me, he doesn't even notice me. Wretched man, I'm fed up with the sight of him. Everyone's talking about our wedding and congratulating us, when there's nothing in it at all actually and the whole thing's so vague.

You've got a brooch that looks like a bee or something.

Anya:
Yes, Mother bought it. Do you know, in Paris, I went up in a balloon.

Chekhov Scenes

<u>Varya:</u>
My lovely, darling Anya's home again.

You know, darling, while I'm doing my jobs around the house I spend the whole day dreaming. I imagine marrying you off to a rich man. That would set my mind at rest and I'd go off to a convent, then on to Kiev and Moscow, wandering from one holy place to another. I'd just wander on and on. What bliss!

<u>Anya:</u>
The bird's are singing in the orchard. What time is it?

<u>Varya:</u>
It must be nearly three. Time you were asleep, dear.

What bliss!

Chekhov Scenes

THREE SISTERS ACT 1

(This is the opening scene of the play. Olga is reminiscing about the past and the fact that her father died exactly one year ago. Olga is dressed in her school teaching clothes. She is talking to her younger sister, Irina, who is dressed in white)

Olga:
It's been exactly one year since Father died – on your name day, Irina. It was bitter cold, snowing, remember? I didn't think I'd ever get through it. And you, you fainted dead away. But now a year has passed and it's easier to talk about. And you are wearing white again and you look radiant. (*She listens as the clock strikes*). The clock was striking then too. Remember, how the band was playing when they took father to the cemetery, how they fired a graveside salute? Hardly anyone came to the funeral and here he was a general, the commander of the brigade. Of course, it was raining and snowing heavily at the time.

Irina:
Why bring up old memories?

Olga:
It's so warm we can have the windows open and yet there is not a single bud on the birch trees. Eleven years ago, when father was given command of the brigade, we all came here from Moscow. I can remember perfectly the beginning of May in Moscow. By this time in Moscow everything's in full bloom, and it's warm – everything is bathed in sunlight. Eleven years have passed. But I remember everything as if we'd left yesterday. Oh, dear God! When I woke up this morning and saw the sunlight everywhere, I knew right away it was spring time, and I felt my heart would burst with joy! I wanted so much to go home again.

(*She hears Masha whistling*)

Don't whistle Masha. How can you? (*Pause*) After teaching High School all day and then giving private lessons till dinner, I have a constant headache. And my thought – I've even started thinking like an old woman. In fact, for the past four years I've worked at the High School, every day I've felt my strength, my youth being drained off drop by drop. Only one thing, one dream keeps me strong, keeps me going ... Moscow!

Irina:
To go to Moscow, to sell the house, have done with everything here and go to Moscow.

Olga:
Yes, to Moscow! As soon as we can.

Irina:
Andrei's probably going to be a professor and he won't live here anyway. There's nothing stopping us except poor Masha here.

Olga:
Masha can come and spend the whole summer in Moscow every year.

Irina:
I only pray it will work out all right. What a marvelous day! I'm in such a good mood, I don't know why. This morning I remembered it was my name-day and I suddenly felt happy, I remembered when we were children and Mother was still alive. And such wonderful thoughts passed through my head, I felt so excited.

Olga:
You're perfectly radiant today, I've never seen you look so beautiful. Masha's beautiful too. Andrei wouldn't be bad-looking either, only he's put on so much weight and it doesn't suit him. But I've aged and grown terribly thin – because I'm always losing my temper with the girls at school, I suppose. Now I have the day off, I'm here at home, my headache's gone and I feel younger than I did yesterday. I'm twenty-eight, that's all. God's in his heaven, all's right with the world, but I think if I got married and stayed at home all day it might be even better. (*Pause*) I'd love my husband.

THREE SISTERS ACT 3

(Irina is feeling depressed and feels she will never get to Moscow or meet the man of her dreams).

Irina:
It's true, how small minded our Andrei has become. How he's wasted himself and grown old, living with that woman! There was a time when he was aiming to be a professor, but now, only yesterday he was boasting that he's at last managed to be elected as a member of the local district council. He's a member of the council, and Protopopov is chairman … the whole town is talking about it and laughing at him, but he is the only one who knows nothing and sees nothing … Just now everyone ran to help to fight the fire, but he sat alone in his study and did not give it a thought. He just plays on the violin. It's terrible, terrible, terrible! (*She cries*) It's too much for me, I can't bear it any longer! … I can't, I can't …. (*She sobs bitterly*).

Olga:
But what's the matter, darling?

Irina:
Don't have anything more to do with me, don't, don't, I can't bear it any longer! (*Sobbing*). Where? Where has it all gone? Where is it? Oh my God, my God! I have forgotten everything, forgotten everything … Everything is confused in my head … I can't remember what is the word for window in Italian, for ceiling … I am forgetting everything. I forget more everyday, and life flies past and never returns, never, and we will never go to Moscow … I see now that we will never go …. (*gaining some control*).

Olga:
Don't, dear, don't.

Irina:
Oh, I'm so unhappy … I can't work, I won't work. That's enough! That's enough! I worked in the Telegraph Office, now I am employed by the Town Council, and I hate and despise everything that they give me to do …

Chekhov Scenes

I'm already twenty four, I have been working already for ages, my brain is drying up, I'm growing ugly and old, and nothing I do, nothing at all gives me any joy, and time goes flying by and all the time it seems as if you are abandoning real life, life that is beautiful, you are going farther and farther away from it, over some sort of precipice. I am in total despair, and how I am alive, why I have not killed myself before now I do not understand… I won't cry, I won't cry… That's enough! …Look, I've already stopped crying. That's enough… that's enough! I kept on waiting, thinking we would settle in Moscow, and there my ideal man would meet me, I dreamed about him, I love him …But it turns out it was all nonsense, all nonsense ….

<u>Olga:</u>
Don't cry, child, please, it upsets me so.

<u>Irina:</u>
I'm not crying. I'm not. I won't. Look, I've stopped now. I must stop, I really must.

<u>Olga:</u>
My dear, let me tell you something as your sister and your friend. If you want my advice, marry the baron.

(Irina continues crying)

After all you do respect him, you think so much of him. He may not be all that good-looking, but he's a fine, decent man. One doesn't marry for love, you know, it's only a matter of doing one's duty. That's what I think anyway, and I'd marry without love. I'd marry the first man who came along provided it was someone honest and decent. I'd even marry an old man.

<u>Irina:</u>
I've been waiting for us to move to Moscow all this time, thinking I'd meet my true love there. I've dreamed about him, loved him, but that was sheer foolishness as it's turned out.

Olga:
I understand, Irina darling, I do understand. When the baron resigned his commission and came to see us in his civilian suit, he looked so ugly it actually brought tears to my eyes. He asked me why I was crying. How could I tell him? But if he did marry you, if such was God's will, I'd be happy. That's an altogether different thing, you see.

ABOUT THE AUTHOR

Kim Gilbert trained as a professional actress at the Guildford School of Acting, Guildhall School of Music and Drama and at the Open University. She has been acting, teaching and directing plays and musical productions for more than 35 years. She has experience in a wide range of theatre, TV and voiceover work. She has a First-class Honours degree in English and has taught English and Drama in many top schools in the country. Kim has examined for Lamda for a number of years and has been running Dramatic Arts Studio for 11 years, a private drama studio which specialises in developing excellence in all forms of performance and communication.

www.dramaticartsstudio.com

Other Books by the same author:

<u>Shakespeare Scenes</u>

Monologues for young female actors
Monologues for young adult female actors
Duologues for female actors
Monologues for young male actors

<u>Scenes from Oscar Wilde</u>

Monologues & Duologues for female actors

Available from Amazon Bookstore

"Thanks for reading! If you enjoyed this book or found it useful, I'd be very grateful if you'd post a short review on Amazon. Your support really does make a difference and I read all the reviews personally so I can get your feedback and make this book even better.

Thanks again for your support!"

Printed in Great Britain
by Amazon